COZY MYSTERY
COLORING BOOK

I created this coloring book as nothing more than for the enjoyment of my readers. They are crafting aficionados, super sleuths, and clever beyond measure when it comes to solving crimes that happen in small towns. These are never faceless big city murders, but the church organist, or the grumpy shop keeper and every character plays a part or provides a red herring. My readers keep me writing, so thank you to you all and I hope you love this as much as I loved the creativity of making it.
Stella

stellaberrybooks.com

"Cozy mysteries are like comfort food for the curious mind."
— Cleo Coyle

"The art of sleuthing is best enjoyed with a cup of tea and a good friend."
— Maggie Sefton

Tea, knitting, and a dash of murder make for an irresistible story

"The amateur sleuth proves that you don't need a badge to bring justice to your community."
— Nancy Atherton

Cozy is a bookshop

"Even the most serene places hold secrets that can shake their tranquility."
— Cleo Coyle

"In quaint villages, the most extraordinary adventures unfold behind the most ordinary doors."
— Louise Penny

"Cornish Cream Tea
with a dollop of death
on the side."
— Stella Berry

"Unraveling mysteries in charming locales adds a touch of magic to the mundane."
— Agatha Frost

"Even the most serene places hold secrets that can shake their tranquility."
— Cleo Coyle

"A cozy mystery is a literary hug with a hint of homicide."
— Amanda Flower

"Cozy mysteries weave a web of intrigue with threads of everyday life."

— Lea Wait

"The best cozy mysteries wrap you in warmth while keeping you on your toes."
— Jenn McKinlay

"Even the most picturesque settings can harbor dark secrets."
— Julia Spencer-Fleming

"Amidst the bustle of everyday life, the clues to great mysteries lie hidden."

— Nancy J. Cohen

"Some ghosts just don't want to rest in peace!"
— Stella Berry

"Behind the charm of everyday life lies a world of hidden mysteries."
— Dorothy St. James

There's nothing quite like a locked room mystery to get my attention.

My happy place is
Mystery Books,
Coffee & Cats

Nothing happens in a village that the elderly aren't aware of

"The beauty of a cozy mystery lies in its ability to make murder feel like a riddle to be solved."
— Maddie Day

"When the ordinary turns extraordinary, the smallest details unravel the biggest mysteries."
— M.C. Beaton

BED & BREAKFAST

"In cozy mysteries, the sleuth's wit is as sharp as the murderer's knife."
— Agatha Frost

"In cozy mysteries, the setting is as important as the crime."
— Nancy Atherton

There's something about a pretty English village that makes you think ... Murder!

"Amidst tea parties and garden clubs, the scent of mystery lingers."
— Miranda James

Fertilizer

"The most unexpected heroes emerge from the humblest of places."
— Kate Carlisle

"A cozy mystery is a literary hug with a hint of homicide."
— Amanda Flower

In a quiet town, secrets whisper from every corner."
— Vicki Delany

"Solving a cozy mystery is like knitting a pattern; it takes patience and attention to detail."
— Maggie Sefton

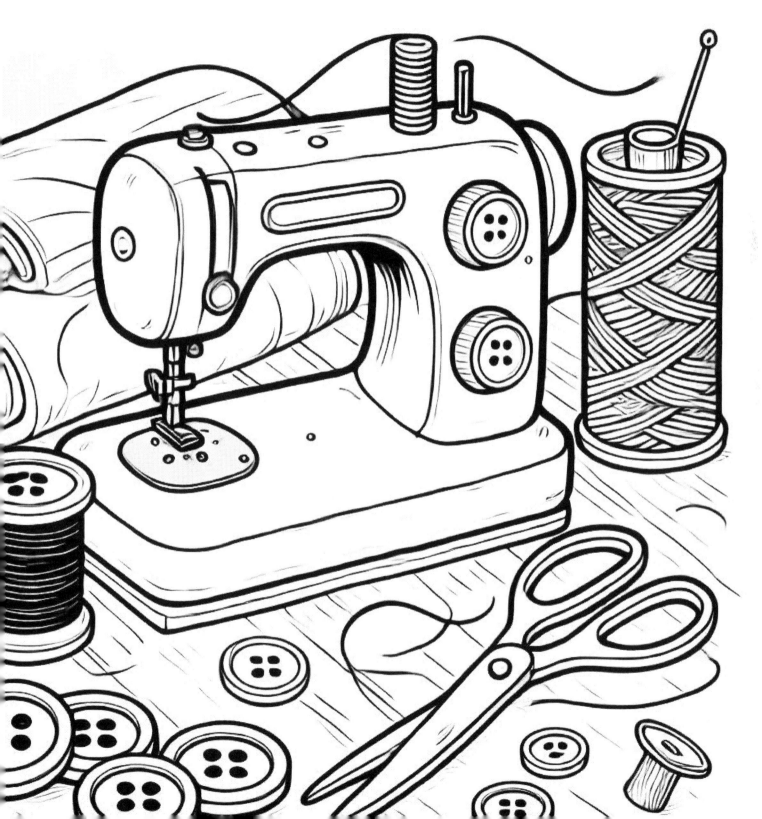

"Behind every charming facade, a deeper story waits to be discovered."
— Leslie Meier

"In a cozy mystery, the dead body is the only cold thing."
— Louise Penny

Small towns always
have the most
interesting characters

"A cozy mystery invites you to solve the crime and stay for the company."
— Laura Childs

"In a cozy mystery, every character has a story, and every story has a clue."
— Elizabeth Spann Craig

A cozy mystery is like a puzzle wrapped in a warm blanket

I hope you enjoyed this cozy mystery coloring book, please do leave a review on Amazon if you did! Thank you :)

Cozy Mystery books by the author:

Murder Most Pumpkin
Body at the Bakery
Murder at the Mansion
Killer at the Castle
Buried at the Bookshop
Fatality at the Christmas Fayre

stellaberrybooks.com

Made in the USA
Monee, IL
27 October 2024